W9-CFJ-435

A ROOKIE READER

JOSHUA JAMES LIKES TRUCKS

By Catherine Petrie

Illustrations by Jerry Warshaw

Prepared under the direction of Robert Hillerich, Ph.D.

CHILDRENS PRESS ™

CHICAGO

For Luke

Library of Congress Cataloging in Publication Data

Petrie, Catherine.
  Joshua James likes trucks.

  (A Rookie reader)
  Summary: A little boy likes all kinds of
trucks. Includes word list.
  [1. Trucks — Fiction]   I. Warshaw, Jerry,
ill.   II. Title.   III. Series.
PZ7.P44677Jo   [E]   81-17076
ISBN O-516-03525-8   AACR2

Joshua James likes trucks.

BIG TRUCKS ...

little trucks ...

7

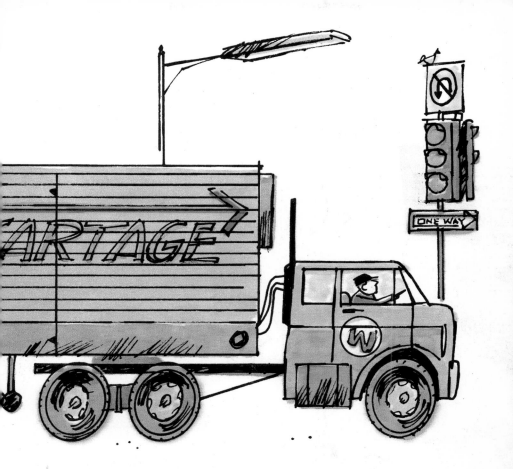

l-o-n-g trucks ...

9

short trucks.

Joshua James just likes trucks!

Red trucks ...

green trucks ...

yellow trucks ...

blue trucks.

Joshua James just likes trucks.

Trucks that go up ...

DETOUR

trucks that go down ...

and trucks that go round and round.

Joshua James just likes trucks.

WORD LIST

and	little
big	long
blue	red
down	round
go	short
green	that
Joshua James	trucks
just	up
likes	yellow

About the Author

Catherine Petrie is a reading specialist with a Master of Science degree in Reading. She has been teaching reading in the public school system for the past ten years. Her experience as a teacher has made her aware of the lack of material currently available for the very young reader. Her creative use of a limited vocabulary based on high-frequency sight words, combined with frequent repetition and rhyming word families, provide the beginning reader with a positive independent reading experience. *Hot Rod Harry, Sandbox Betty,* and *Joshua James Likes Trucks* are her first published beginning readers.

About the Artist

Jerry Warshaw, a native Chicagoan, received his training at the Art Institute of Chicago, the Chicago Academy of Fine Arts, and the Institute of Design.

Mr. Warshaw has pursued a varied free-lance career, including the illustration of the American history comic strip "The American Adventure." He served as Art Consultant to the Illinois Sesquicentennial Commission, and in addition to designing the official Sesquicentennial emblem and flag, designed and illustrated the *ILLINOIS INTELLIGENCER,* the Sesquicentennial Commission's newspaper. His illustrations have appeared in numerous children's books, educational texts, magazines, and advertisements. He also designs posters, greeting cards, and sculpture.

A historian by avocation, Mr. Warshaw is a life member of the Chicago Historical Society, former president of the Civil War Round Table and the Children's Reading Round Table, and a member of the Society of Typographic Arts, the Chicago Press Club, and the Art Institute of Chicago.

Mr. Warshaw lives in Evanston with his wife Joyce, daughter Elizabeth, three cats, a newt, a guinea pig, and two gerbils.